Ivy Bird

Tania McCartney + Jess Racklyeft

BLUE DOT KIDS PRESS

For my darling Ella, too soon ready to leave the nest.
— Tania McCartney

To Ivy, thank you for teaching me again how to talk to birds.
— Jess Racklyeft

Ivy Bird

Blue Dot Kids Press
www.BlueDotKidsPress.com
Original North American edition published in 2020 by Blue Dot Kids Press,
PO Box 2344, San Francisco, CA 94126, Blue Dot Kids Press is a trademark of Blue Dot Publications LLC.

Original North American edition © 2020 Blue Dot Publications LLC
Text © 2019 Tania McCartney
Illustrations © 2019 Jess Racklyeft
Various collage textures by Lera Efremov
Original Australian edition published by Windy Hollow Books,
PO Box 265, East Kew, Victoria, Australia 3102

This North American edition is published under exclusive license with Windy Hollow Books.
Original North American edition designed by Susan Szecsi

BLUE
D T

Cataloging in Publication Data is available from the United States Library of Congress.
ISBN: 978-1-7331212-1-7

MIX
Paper from
responsible sources
FSC™ C136333

FSC
www.fsc.org

Printed in China with soy inks.
First Printing

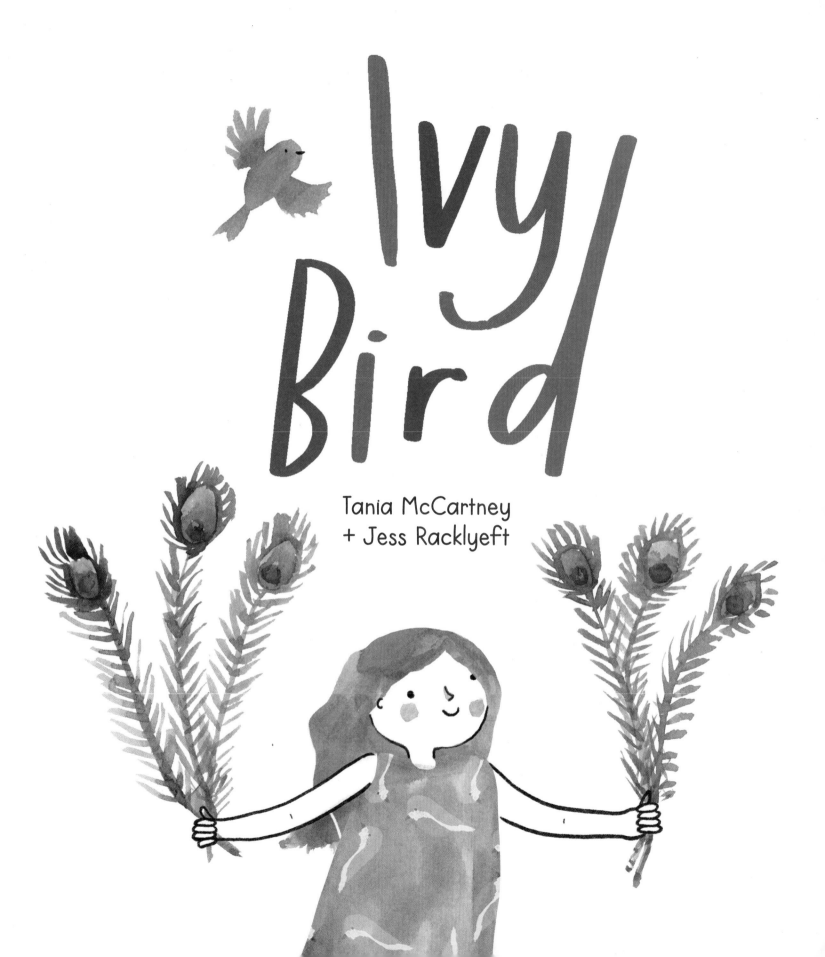

Ivy Bird

Tania McCartney
+ Jess Racklyeft

When the sun comes up,

Ivy wakes to tweets and cheeps.

A little bit of seed

and Ivy takes flight.

For breakfast, she pecks in the sunshine.

Ivy warbles.
She's after the early worm.

Foraging in cups of sweet nectar

is followed by a little feather-fluffing.

When she jumps in the pond,
the ducks are all in a row.

Ivy is the very best paddler of them all.

Lunch is berry delicious.

There are strawberries

and blackberries

and loganberries too.

Ivy loves hide-and-seek.

She finds the perfect
hiding spot where everything
is blooming and smells
like perfume.

Ivy likes shiny bits and pieces—
she hides them under sticks and stones.

It's her secret treasure nest.

The most playful birds call their friends,
then flap their wings

and play tag in the clouds.

Ivy has a lovely voice. She can trill and chirp, peep and chatter, cackle, tweet, and squawk.

All the birds join in.

After dinner,
the bird bath is filled,

and a bright little chick
splashes the day away.

When the sun goes to bed, Ivy's eyes are wide.
She hoots in the dark.

The moon sails high,
and it's time to settle in her nest.

After all, every little bird needs
a place to call home.

Ivy sees many birds during her day of adventure: some in the world around her and some in her imagination. Can you find these birds hidden in the pages of the story?

Canary

Canaries are very friendly, and they love to sing. The males sing the most and have the prettiest voices. Canaries come in many colors.

Magpie

Magpies make a variety of amazing sounds. The birds are unusual because they walk instead of hop.

Hummingbird

A hummingbird's wings beat very, very fast—up to 5,400 times every minute! They are also the only birds that can fly backward.

Duck

Ducks are friendly and curious creatures. They love to dive for their dinner and have a waterproof coating on their feathers to keep them warm and dry.

Robin

Robins are gray or brown, with bright-red tummies, and males are brighter than females. In winter, robins fluff up their feathers to keep out the cold.

Lyrebird

The lyrebird has the most amazing vocal range of all birds—and can mimic other animals, people, car alarms, and even explosions!

Peacock

Peacocks are clever birds. The male has long, glamorous tail feathers, which he shimmies and shakes, hoping to attract a girlfriend!

Bowerbird

Bowerbirds collect little bits and pieces like wire and bottle caps, and most especially anything blue. They have beautiful violet-blue eyes.

Lorikeet

Lorikeets can be very noisy! They love to play and dash from tree to tree, screeching as they go. Their tongues have a little tuft on the end, like a paintbrush!

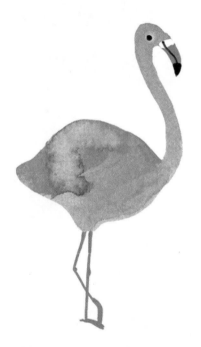

Flamingo

The flamingo's feathers can be white or all kinds of pink and red, depending on what it eats! When it wants to rest, it stands on one leg.

Rosella

Rosellas are a kind of parrot, and there are many different species. They love to bathe in water and can make quite a splashy mess!

Owl

Owls can't move their eyes, so they need to move their heads to look at something. This is why they can turn their heads almost all the way around!